MO AND JO

FIGHTING TOGETHER FOREVER

JAY LYNCH & DEAN HASPIEL

Visit us at www.abdopublishing.com

Reinforced library bound editions published in 2014 by Spotlight, a division of the ABDO Group, PO Box 398166, Minneapolis, MN 55439. Spotlight produces high-quality reinforced library bound editions for schools and libraries. Published by agreement with Raw Junior, LLC.

Printed in the United States of America, North Mankato, Minnesota.
042013
092013
This book contains at least 10% recycled material.

Library of Congress Cataloging-in-Publication Data
This book was previously cataloged with the following information:

Haspiel, Dean.
Mo and Jo : fighting together forever / Dean Haspiel, Jay Lynch.
p. cm. -- (TOON Books)
Summary: Mo and Jo love the same superhero—but can't stand each other! When the mighty Mojo decides to give his powerful costume to them, Mo and Jo fight so much they rip it in half. Now each twin is only half as strong! Can they find a way to combine their powers, fight the evil Saw-Jaw, and save their town?
[E]--dc22

2007943850

ISBN 978-1-61479-152-2 (reinforced library bound edition)

Spotlight

All Spotlight books are reinforced library bindings and manufactured in the United States of America.

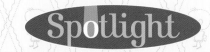

A JUNIOR LIBRARY GUILD SELECTION

For Mom and Dad

–Dean

For Tristan and Seamus

–Jay

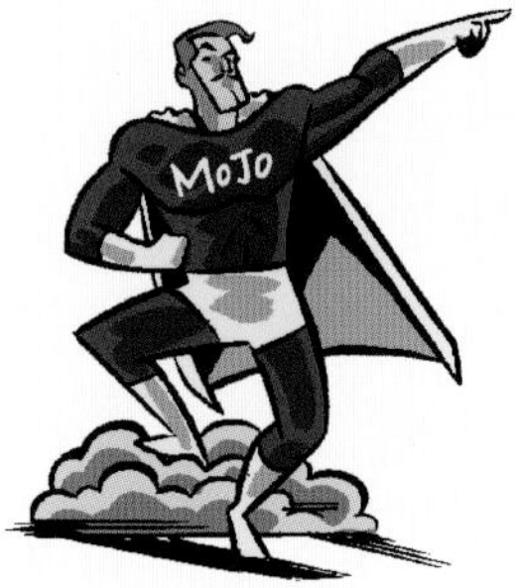
MoJo

Editorial Director: FRANÇOISE MOULY
Advisor: ART SPIEGELMAN

Book Design: FRANÇOISE MOULY & JONATHAN BENNETT

A TOON BOOK

CHAPTER ONE:

FIGHTING...

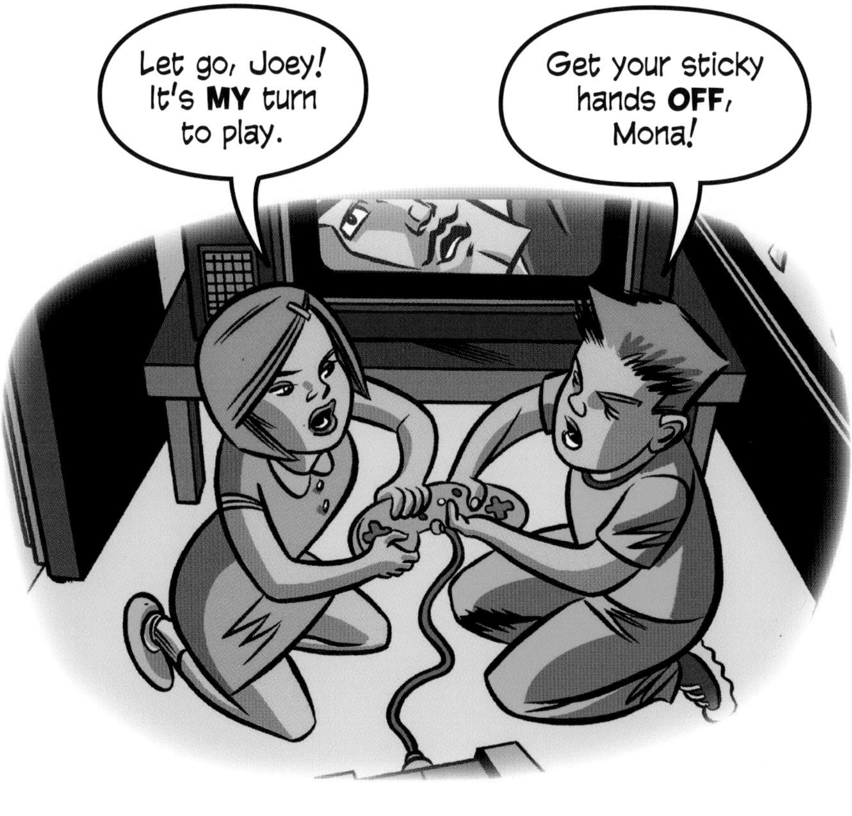
Let go, Joey! It's **MY** turn to play.
Get your sticky hands **OFF**, Mona!

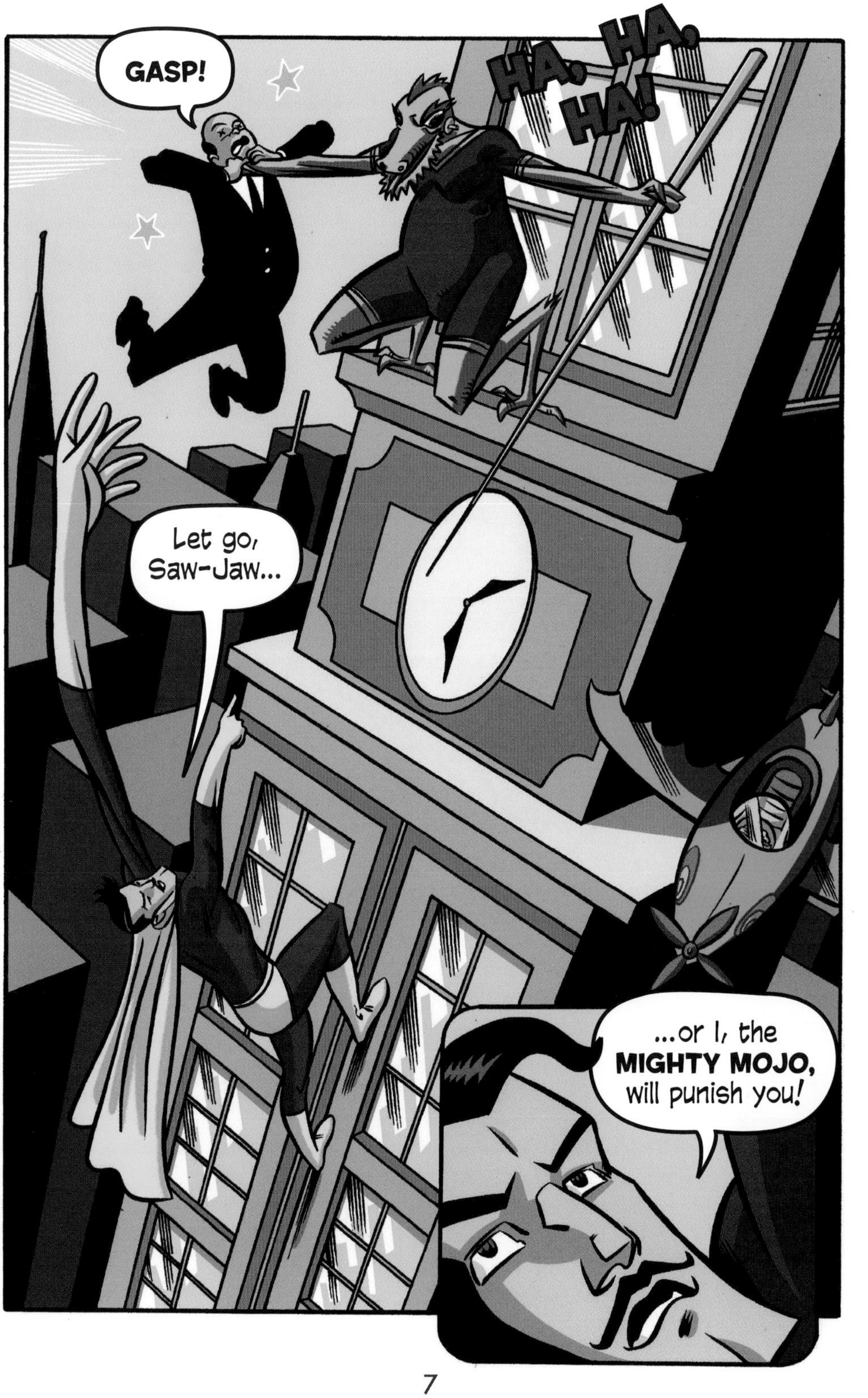
GASP!
HA, HA, HA!
Let go, Saw-Jaw...
...or I, the **MIGHTY MOJO**, will punish you!

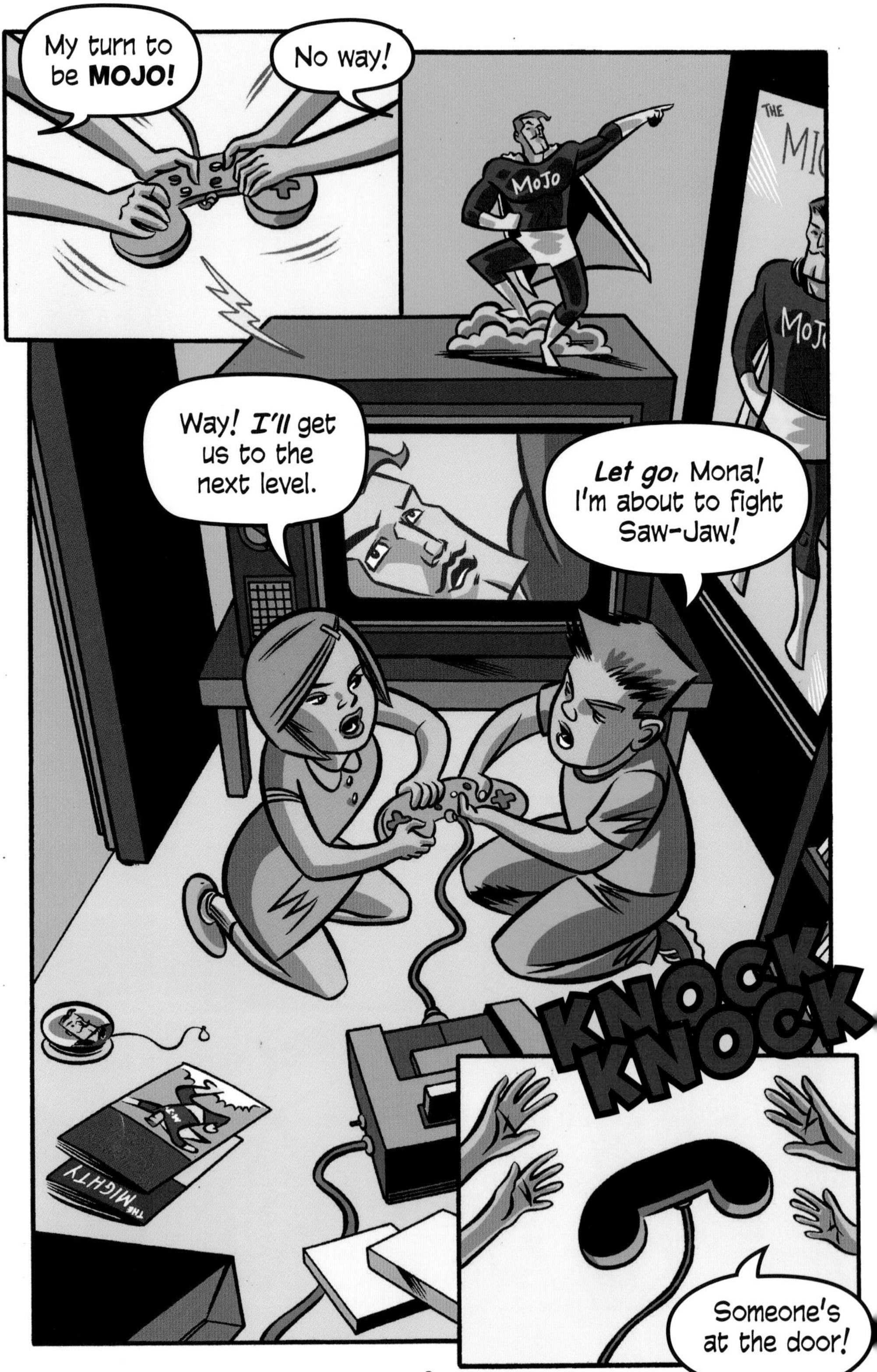

My turn to be **MOJO!**
No way!
MOJO
THE MIG
MOJ
Way! *I'll* get us to the next level.
Let go, Mona! I'm about to fight Saw-Jaw!
KNOCK KNOCK
THE MIGHTY
Someone's at the door!

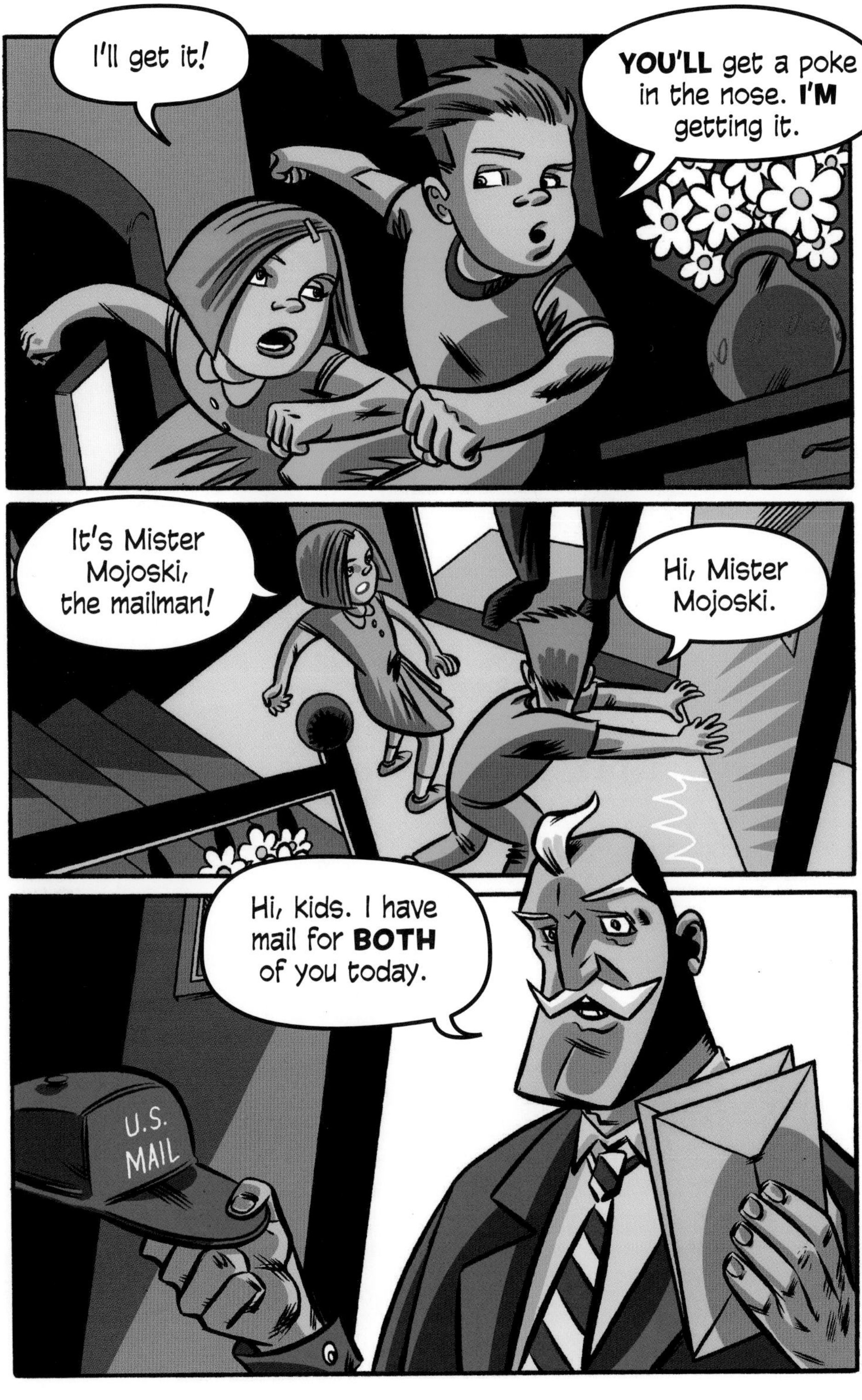
I'll get it!
YOU'LL get a poke in the nose. I'M getting it.
It's Mister Mojoski, the mailman!
Hi, Mister Mojoski.
Hi, kids. I have mail for BOTH of you today.
U.S. MAIL

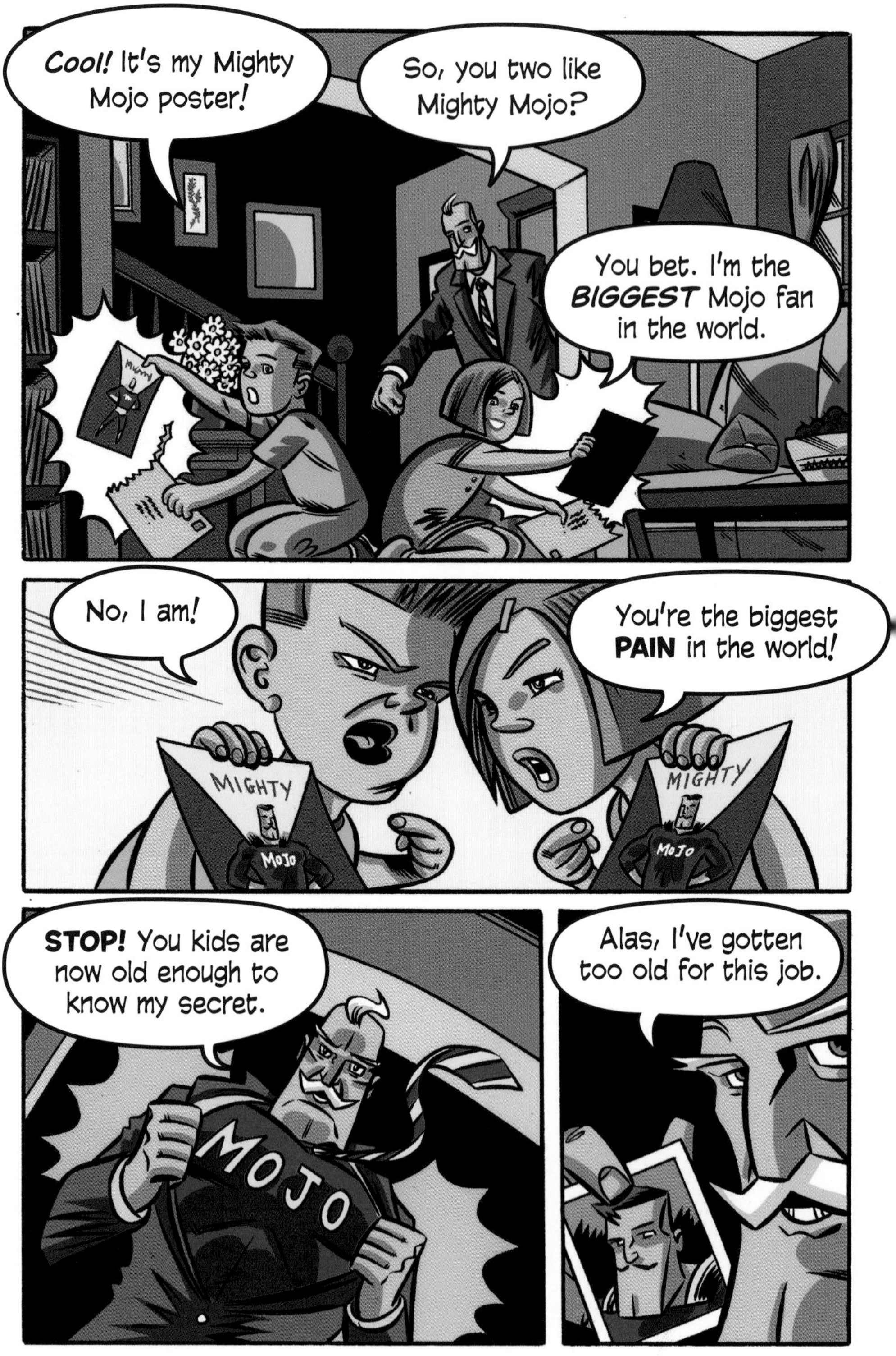
Cool! It's my Mighty Mojo poster!
So, you two like Mighty Mojo?
You bet. I'm the BIGGEST Mojo fan in the world.
MIGHTY
No, I am!
You're the biggest PAIN in the world!
MIGHTY
MOJO
MIGHTY
MOJO
STOP! You kids are now old enough to know my secret.
MOJO
Alas, I've gotten too old for this job.

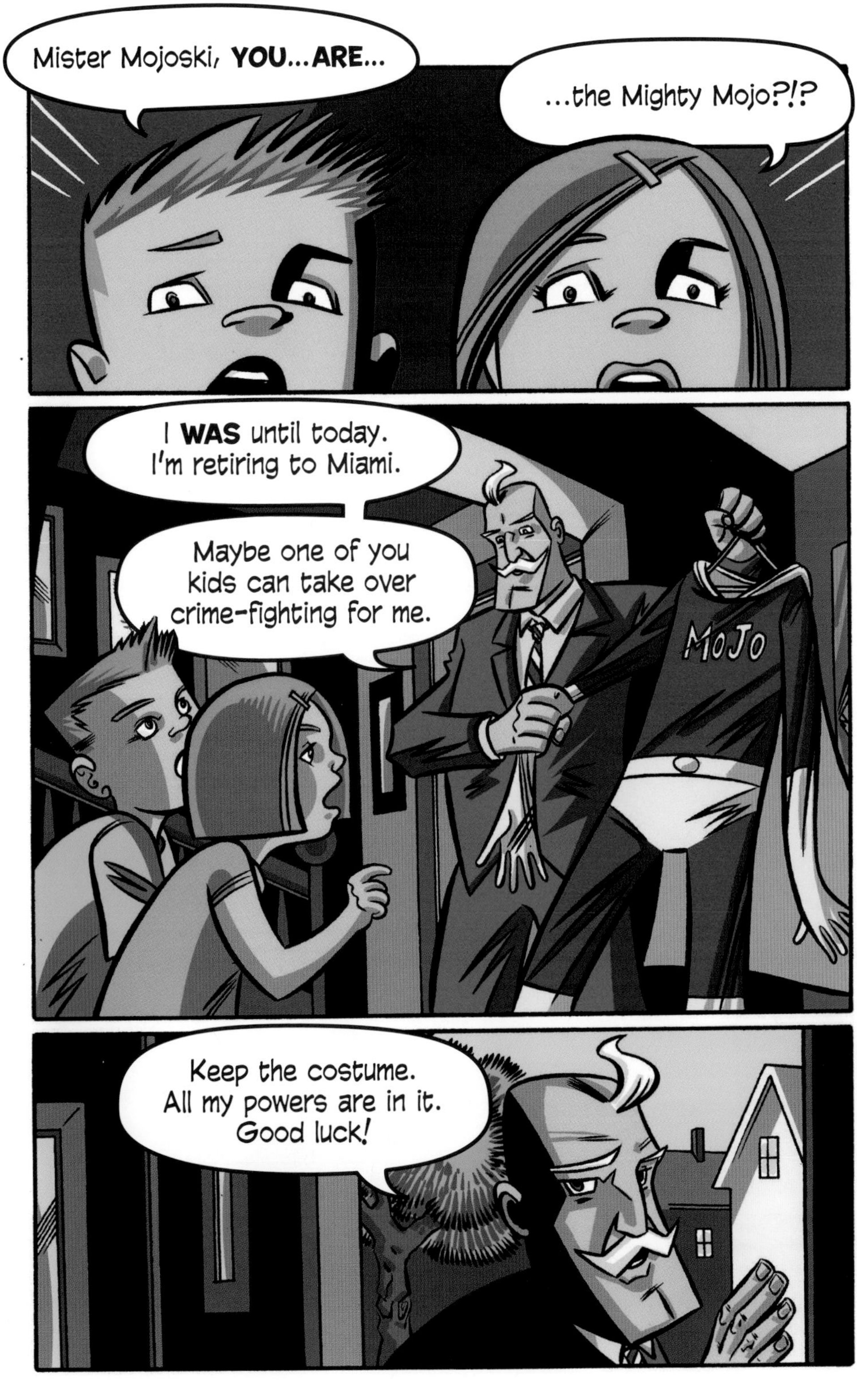
Mister Mojoski, YOU...ARE...
...the Mighty Mojo?!?
I WAS until today. I'm retiring to Miami.
Maybe one of you kids can take over crime-fighting for me.
MoJo
Keep the costume. All my powers are in it. Good luck!

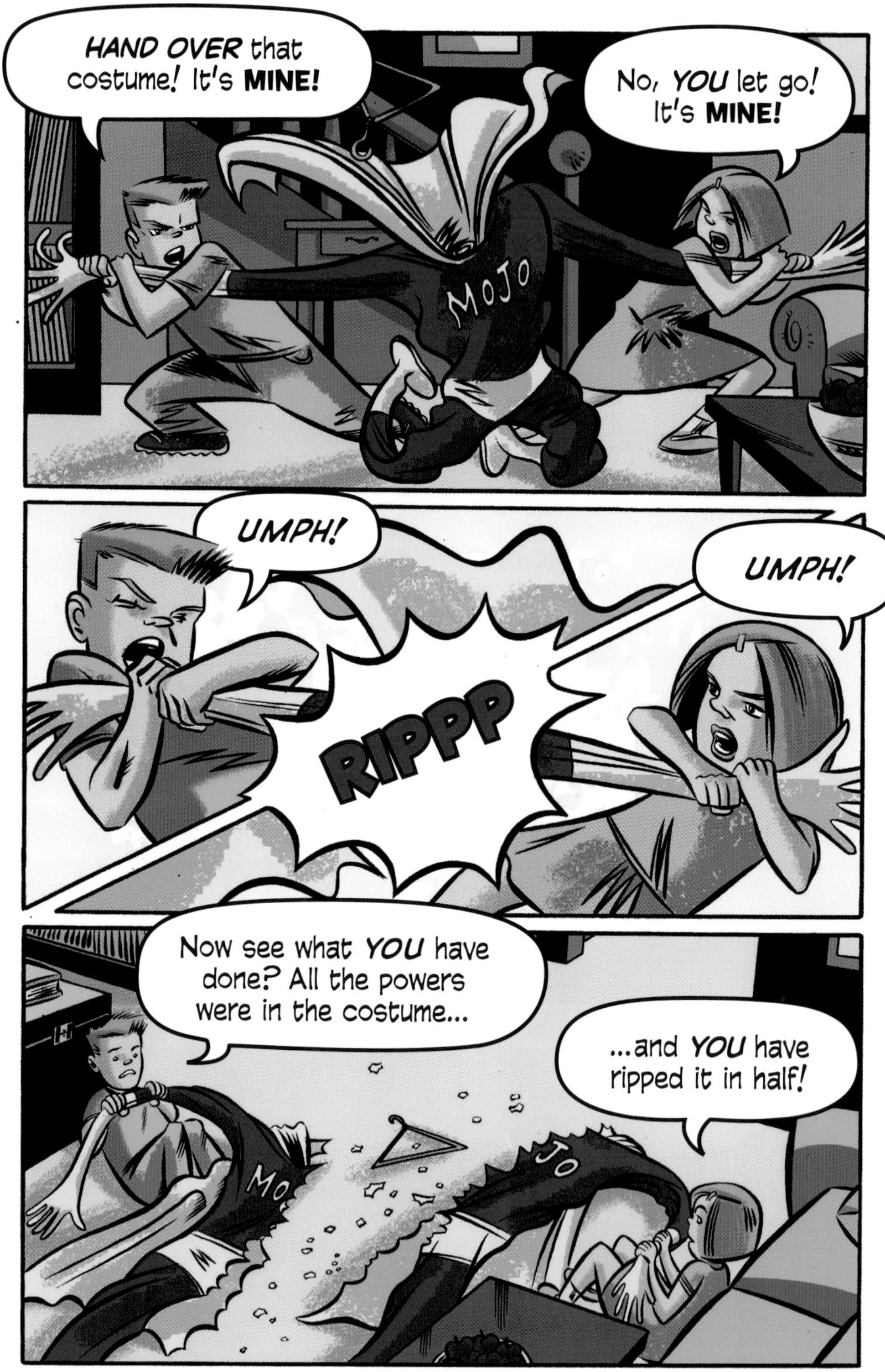
HAND OVER that costume! It's MINE!
No, YOU let go! It's MINE!
MOJO
UMPH!
UMPH!
RIPPP
Now see what YOU have done? All the powers were in the costume...
...and YOU have ripped it in half!
MO
JO

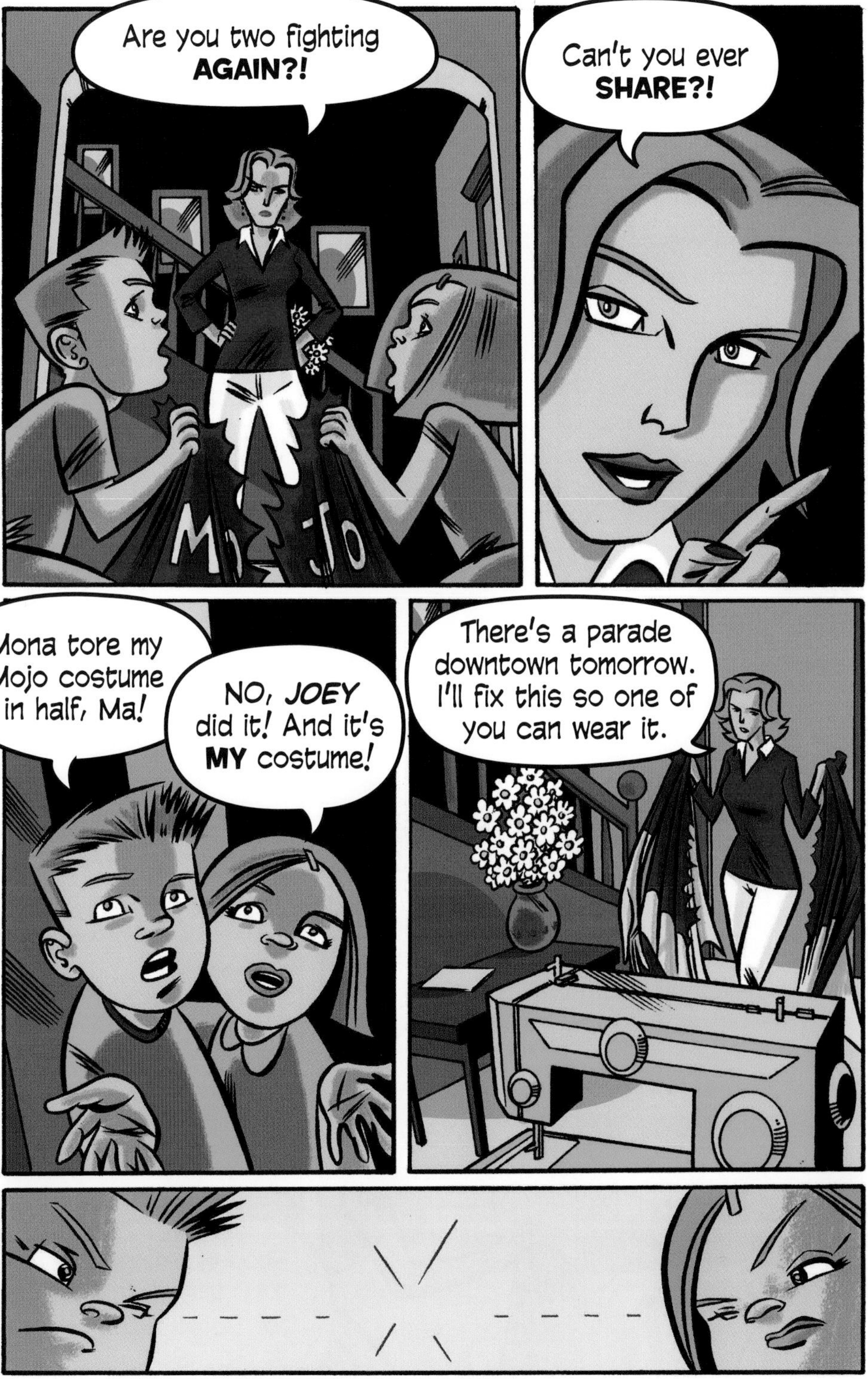
Are you two fighting AGAIN?!
Can't you ever SHARE?!
Mona tore my Mojo costume in half, Ma!
NO, JOEY did it! And it's MY costume!
There's a parade downtown tomorrow. I'll fix this so one of you can wear it.

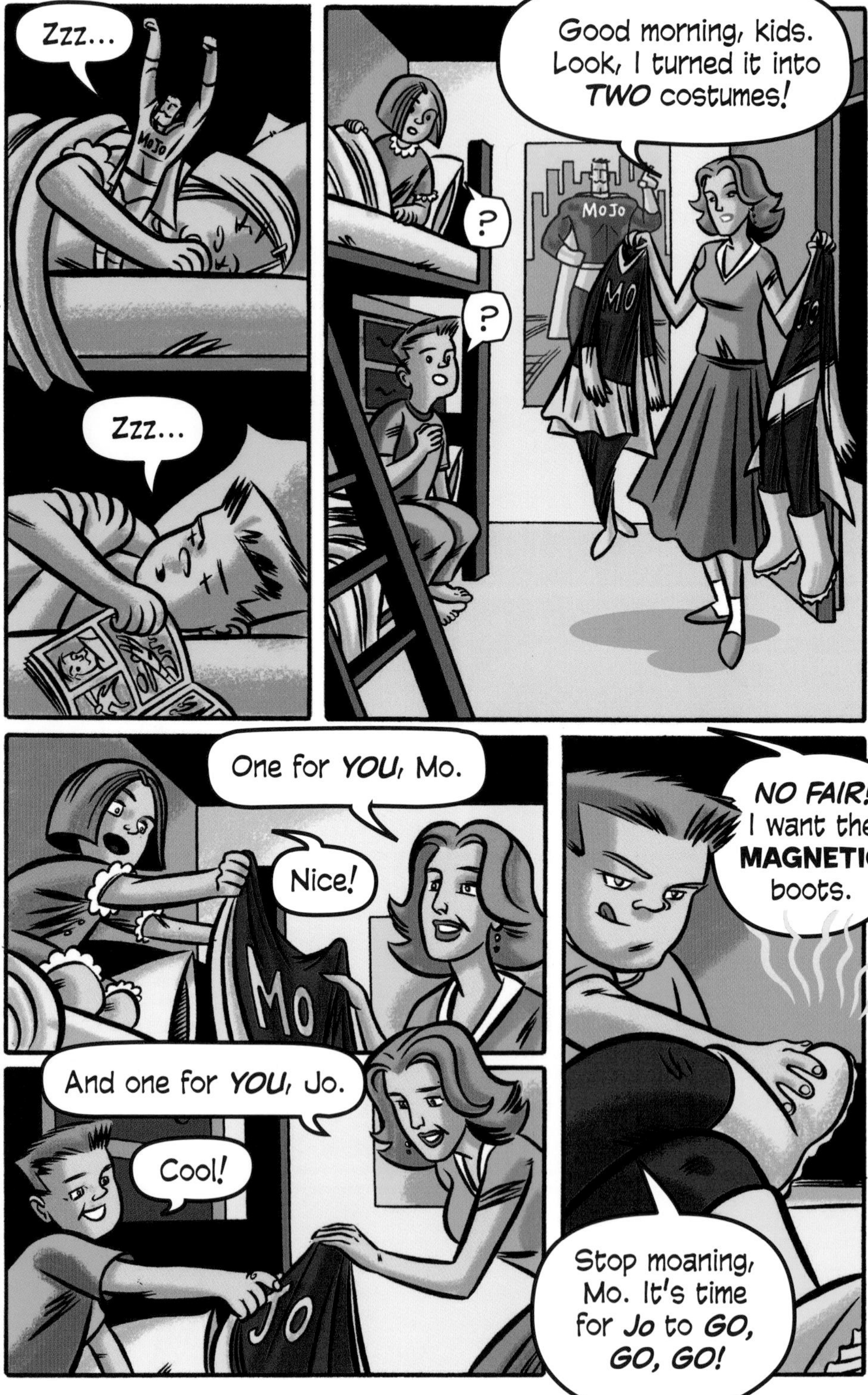
Zzz...
Zzz...
Good morning, kids. Look, I turned it into TWO costumes!
?
?
MOJO
MO
JO
One for YOU, Mo.
Nice!
MO
And one for YOU, Jo.
Cool!
JO
NO FAIR! I want the MAGNETIC boots.
Stop moaning, Mo. It's time for Jo to GO, GO, GO!

CHAPTER TWO:

FIGHTING FOREVER...

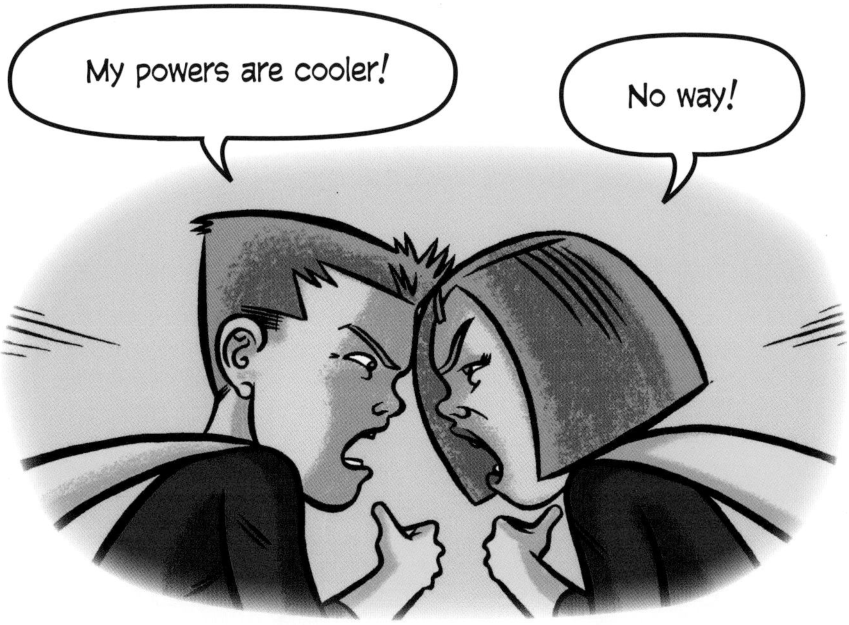
My powers are cooler!
No way!

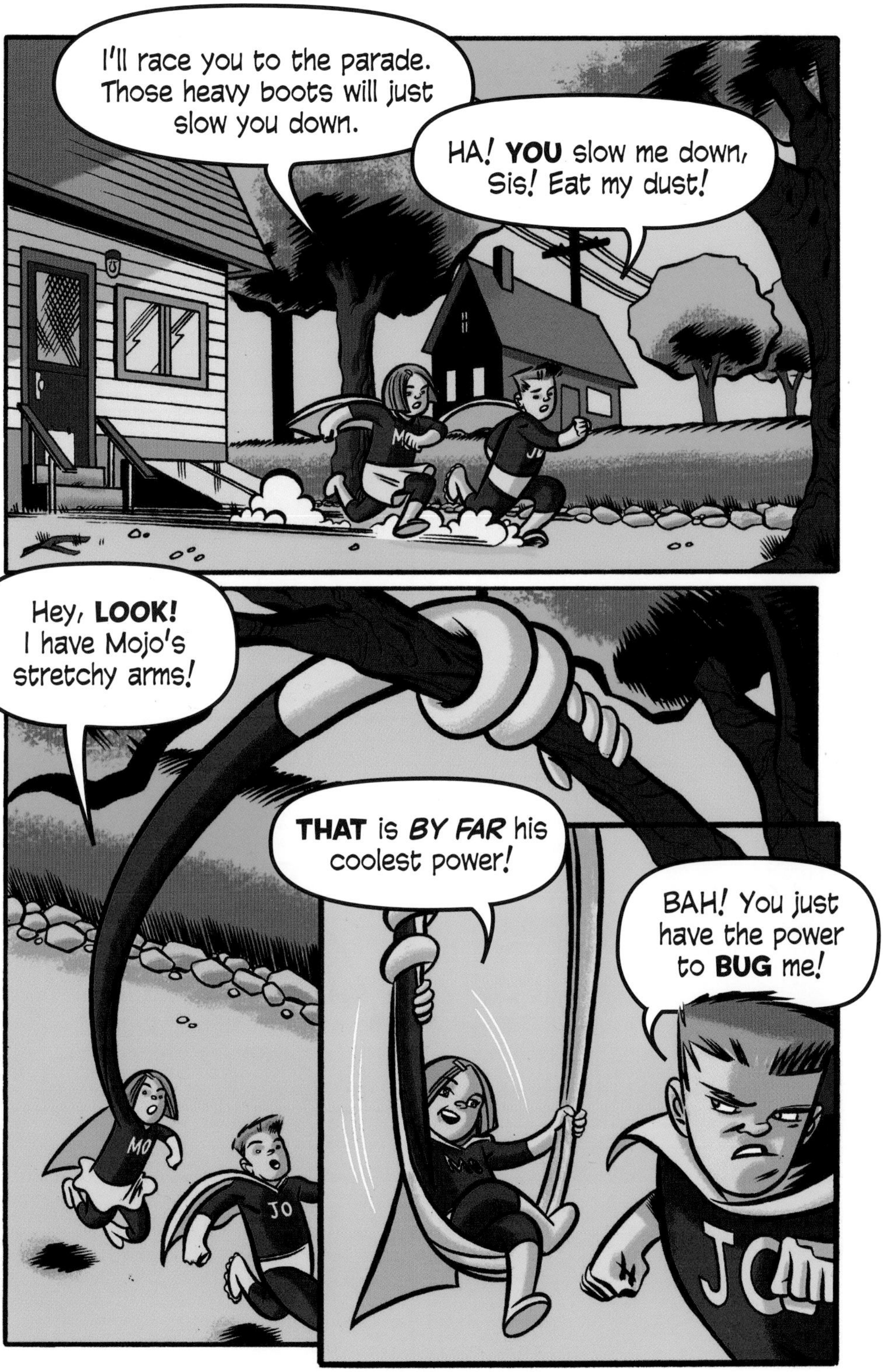
I'll race you to the parade. Those heavy boots will just slow you down.
HA! YOU slow me down, Sis! Eat my dust!
Hey, LOOK! I have Mojo's stretchy arms!
THAT is BY FAR his coolest power!
BAH! You just have the power to BUG me!

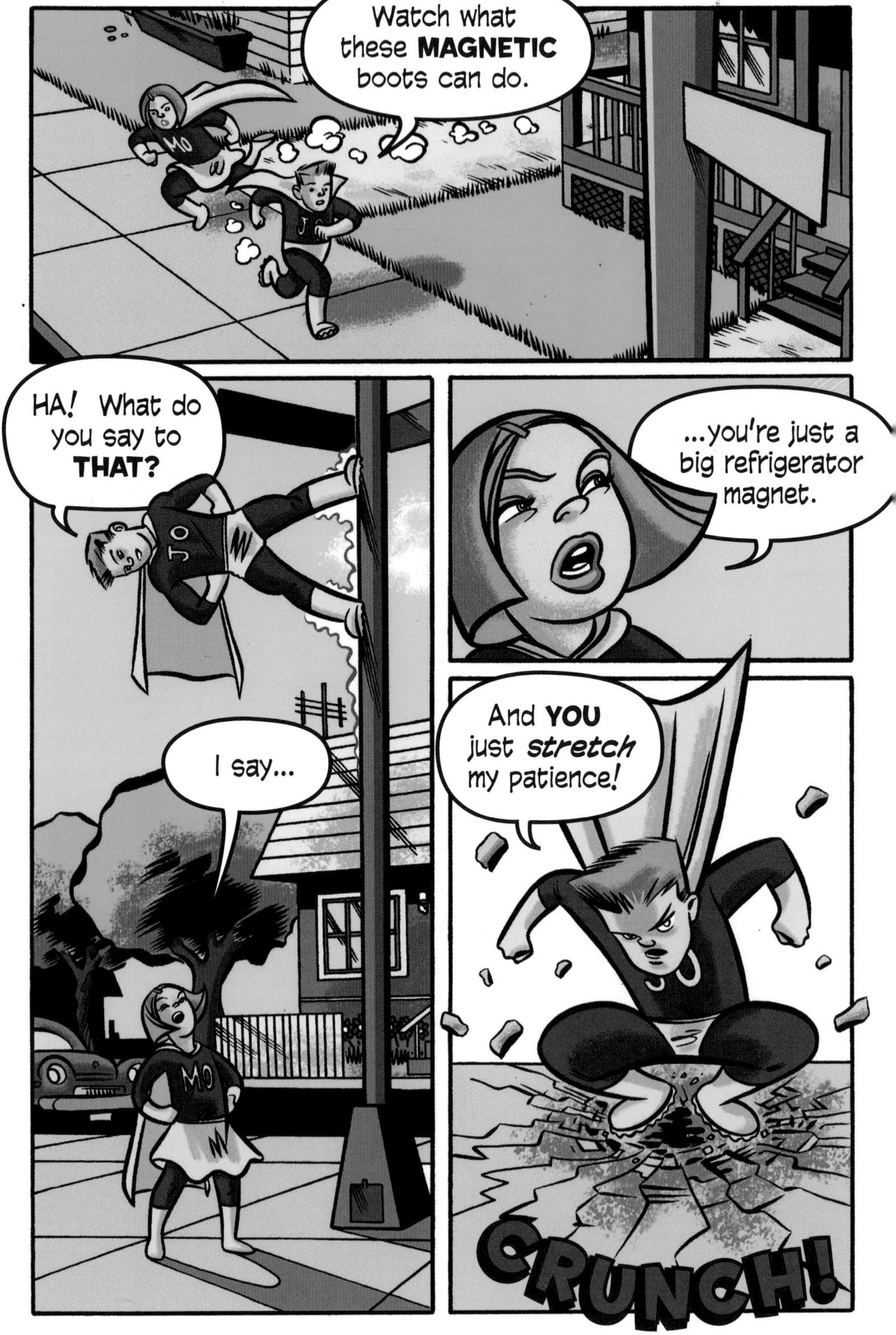
Watch what these **MAGNETIC** boots can do.
HA! What do you say to **THAT?**
I say...
...you're just a big refrigerator magnet.
And **YOU** just *stretch* my patience!
CRUNCH!

19

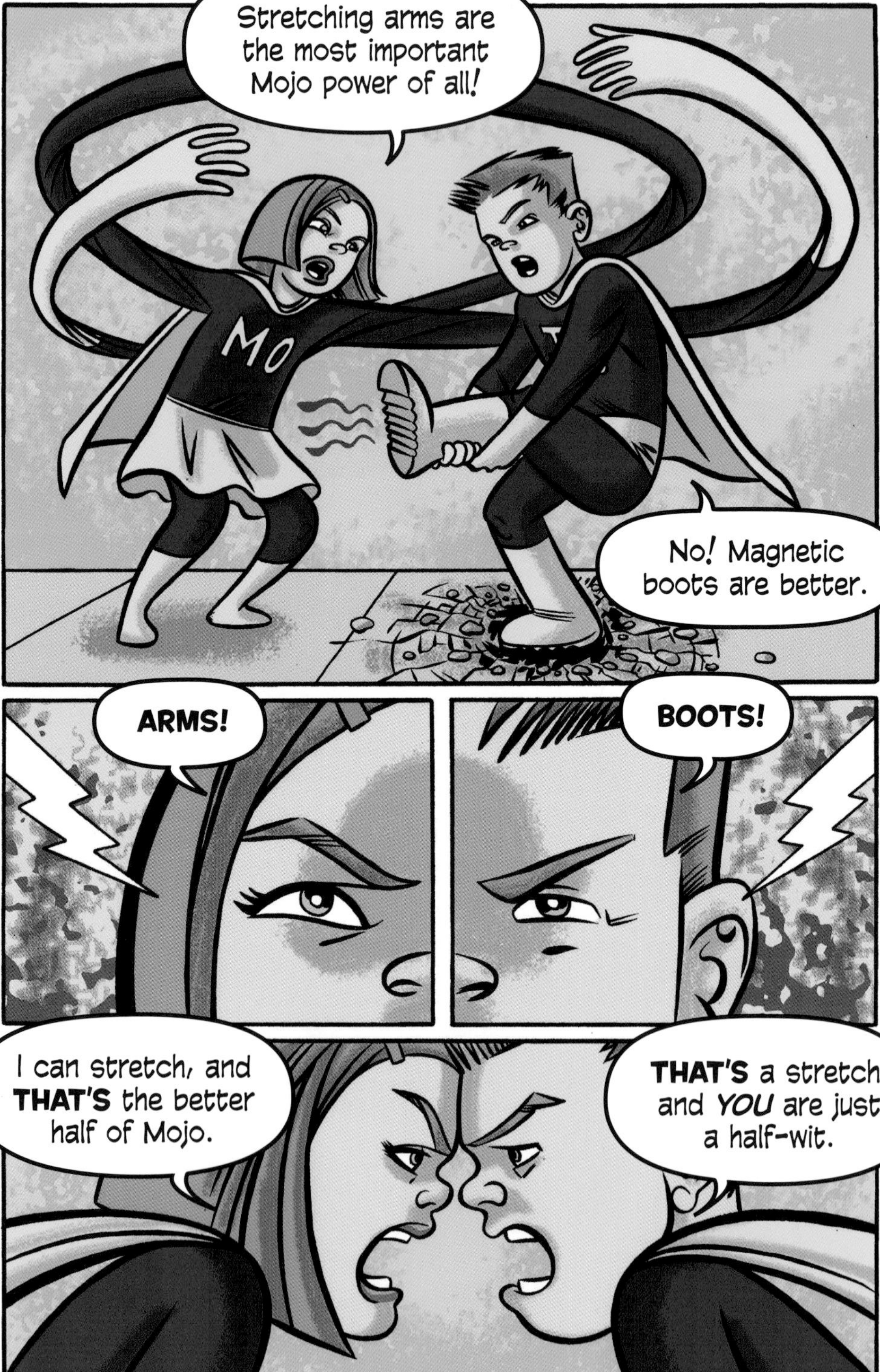
Stretching arms are the most important Mojo power of all!
MO
No! Magnetic boots are better.
ARMS!
BOOTS!
I can stretch, and **THAT'S** the better half of Mojo.
THAT'S a stretch, and *YOU* are just a half-wit.

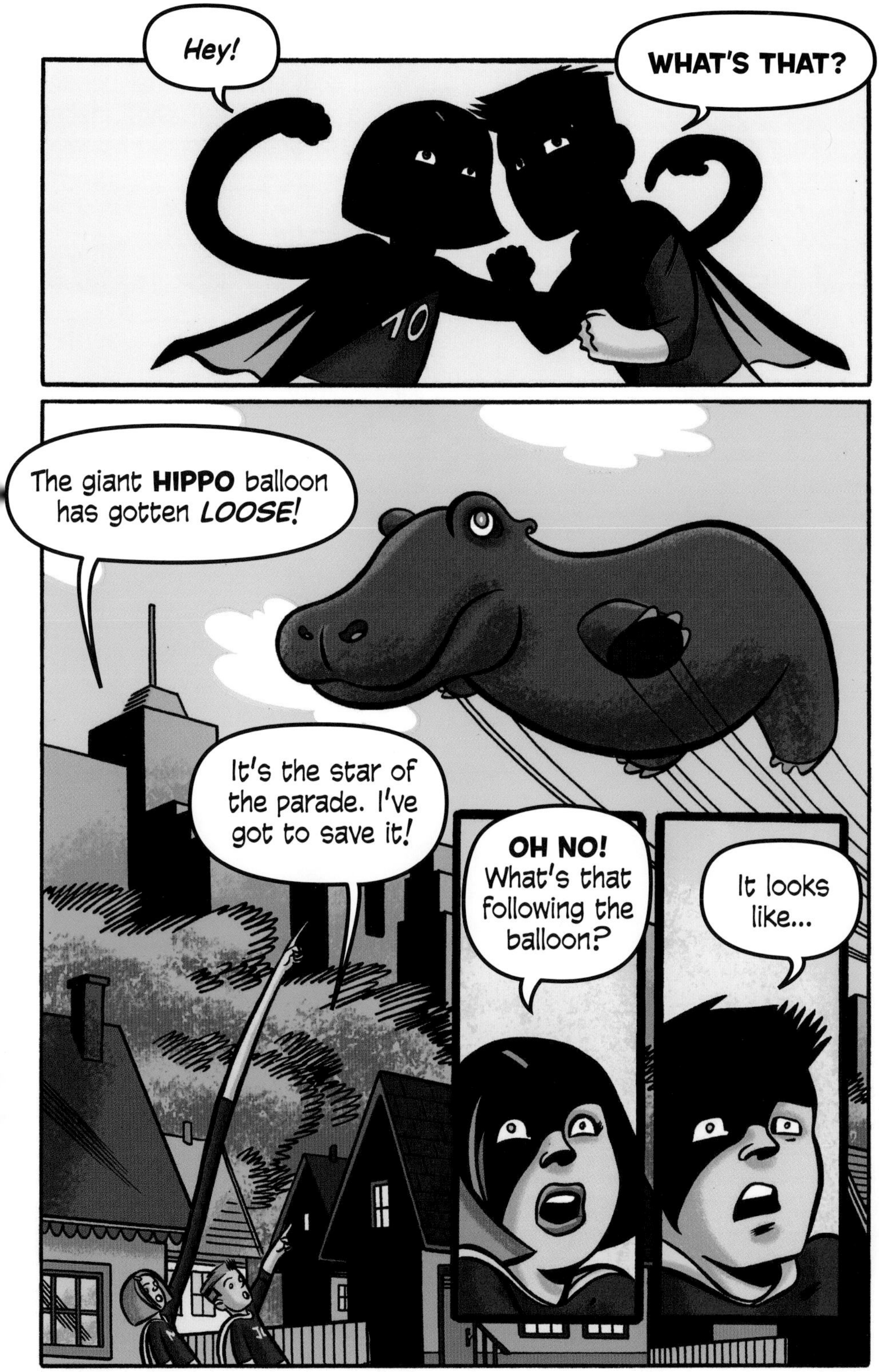
Hey!
WHAT'S THAT?
The giant HIPPO balloon has gotten LOOSE!
It's the star of the parade. I've got to save it!
OH NO! What's that following the balloon?
It looks like...

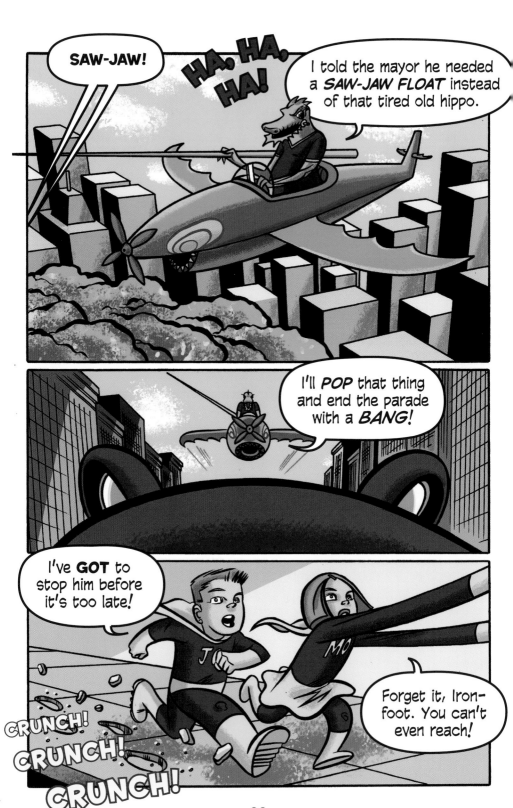

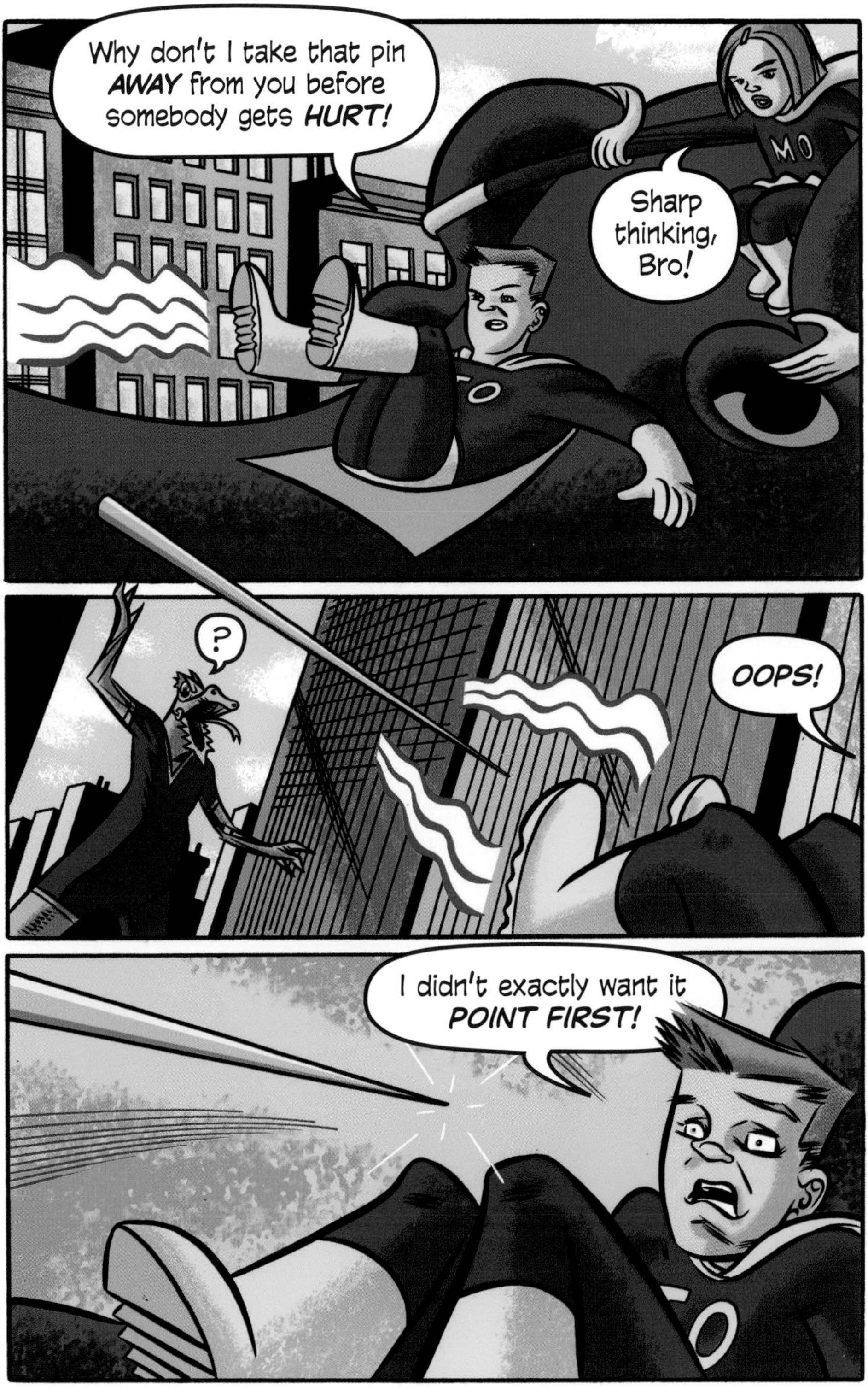
Why don't I take that pin AWAY from you before somebody gets HURT!
Sharp thinking, Bro!
?
OOPS!
I didn't exactly want it POINT FIRST!

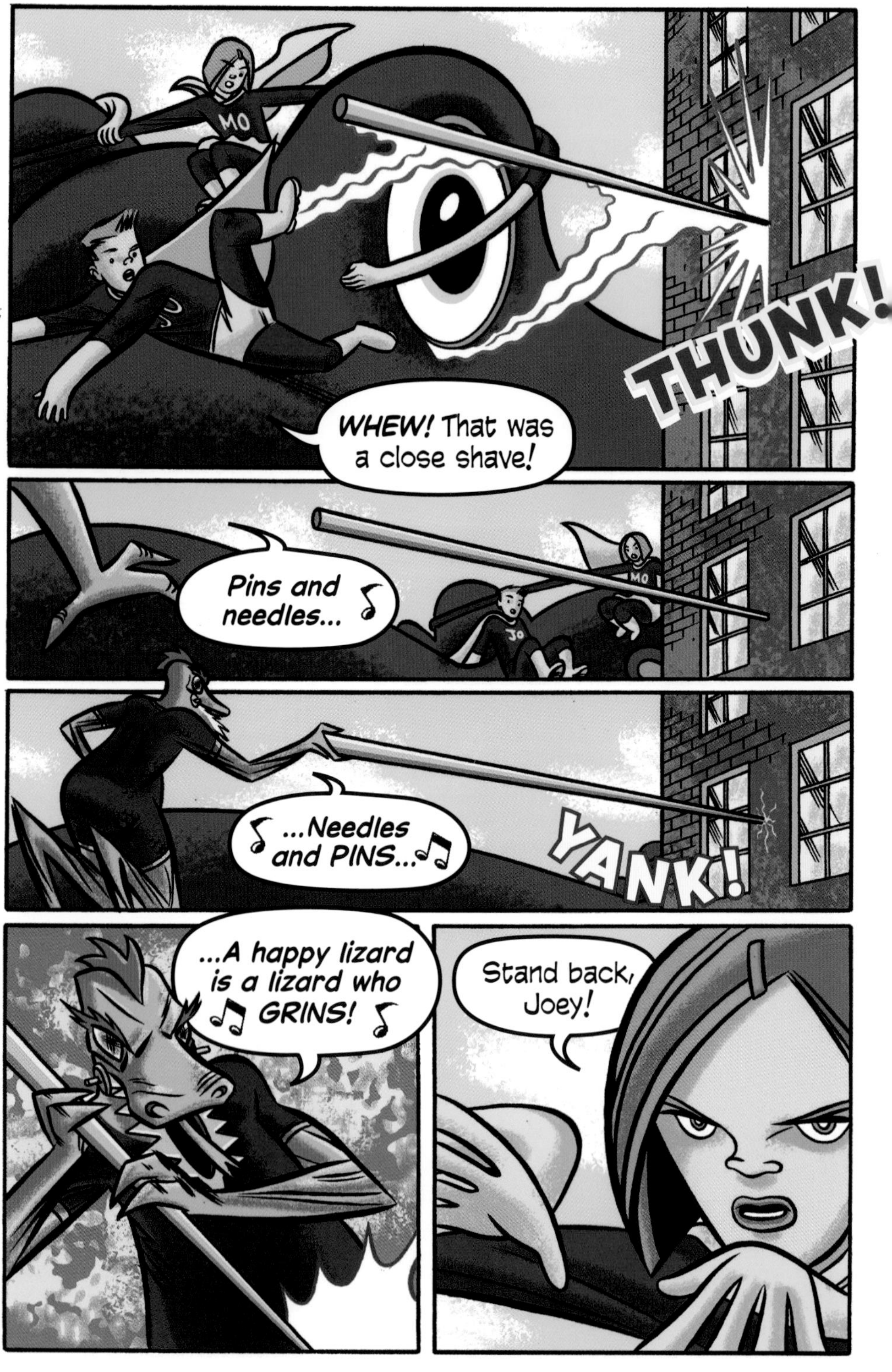
THUNK!
WHEW! That was a close shave!
Pins and needles...
...Needles and PINS...
YANK!
...A happy lizard is a lizard who GRINS!
Stand back, Joey!

CHAPTER THREE:

FIGHTING TOGETHER FOREVER...

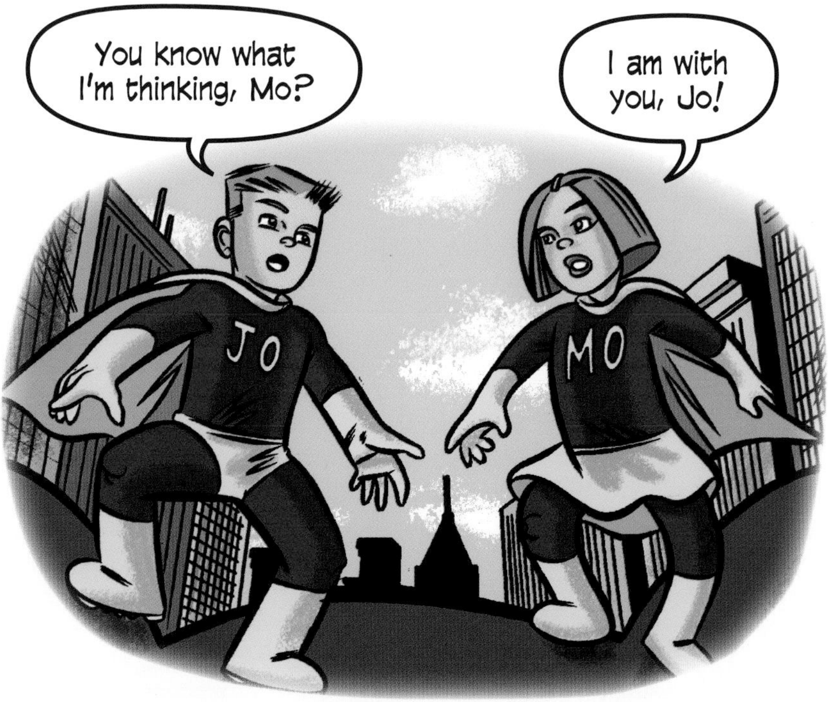
You know what I'm thinking, Mo?
I am with you, Jo!
JO
MO

35

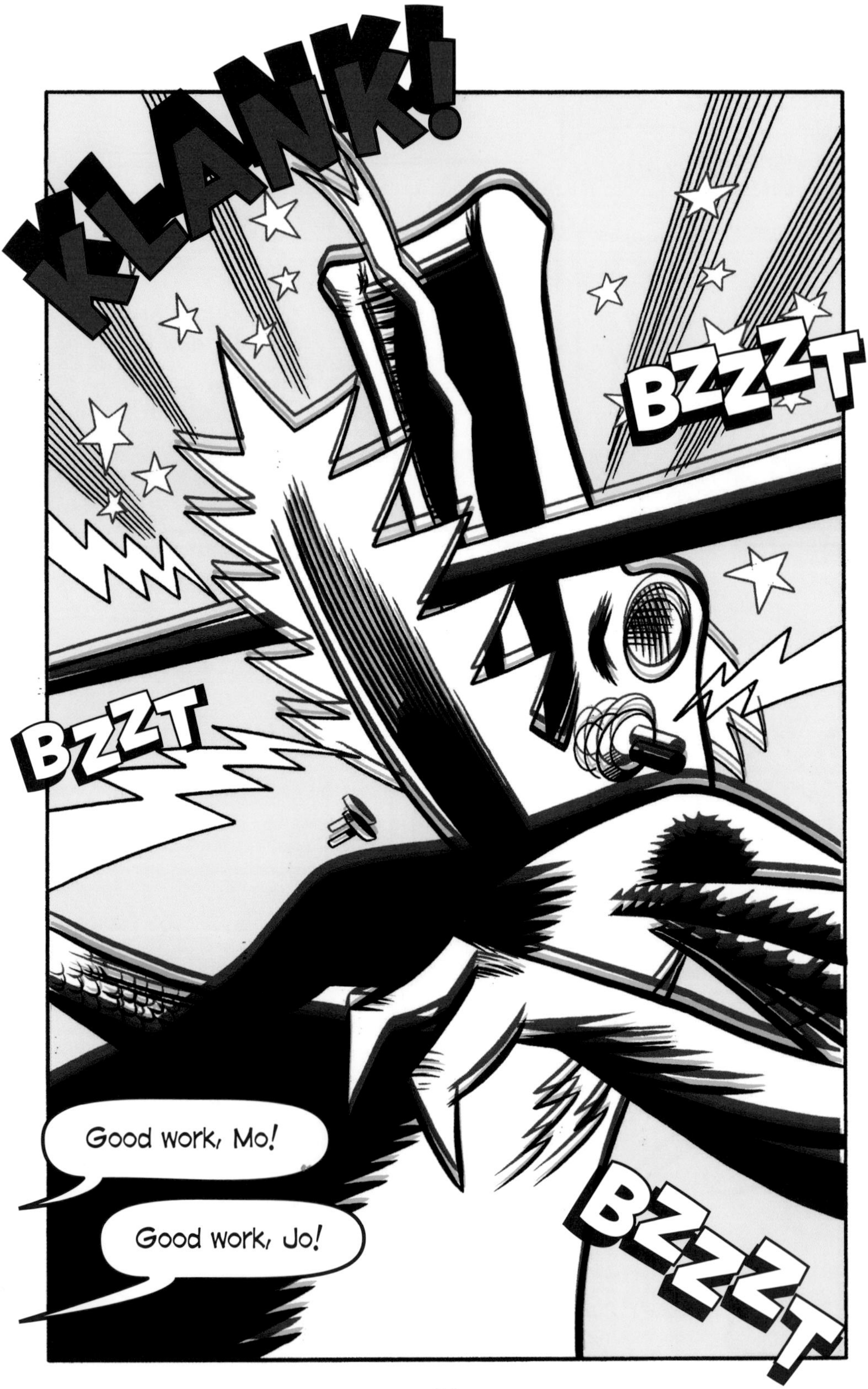
KLANK!
BZZZT
BZZT
Good work, Mo!
Good work, Jo!
BZZZT

Ow!

BOING!

Great job, kids! I've been watching you all along.

That's what happens...

...when we work together as a *TEAM!*

POLICE WAGON

POLICE

THAT'S IT! We'll call ourselves Team **JOMO!**

ER—I think Team **MOJO** sounds *a lot* better!

Yes, Team MOJO! You can be the heroes of the parade!

39

ABOUT THE AUTHORS

JAY LYNCH, who wrote Mo and Jo's story, loved to read funny superhero comics like *Plastic Man* when he was a kid. When he wasn't reading comic books, he would draw his own cartoon characters on the sidewalk in front of his house—then hide in the bushes to hear what other kids had to say about his drawings! Jay grew up to become a legendary cartoonist and has helped create many popular humor products, including *Wacky Packages* and *Garbage Pail Kids.* If he could have any superpower, he'd like to know what color something is just by touching it.

DEAN HASPIEL, who drew Mo and Jo, read *The Fantastic Four* and *Shazam!* when he was a kid. He admits that he used to fight with his brother all the time, too: "All siblings have a healthy rivalry, and so did we." Dean is an Emmy award-winning artist, the founder of the webcomic collective ACT-I-VATE.com, and the illustrator of comics collaborations with Harvey Pekar, Jonathan Ames, and Inverna Lockpez. He also draws for HBO's *Bored To Death.* If he could have any superpower, he'd like to fly, "because that would just be cool!"

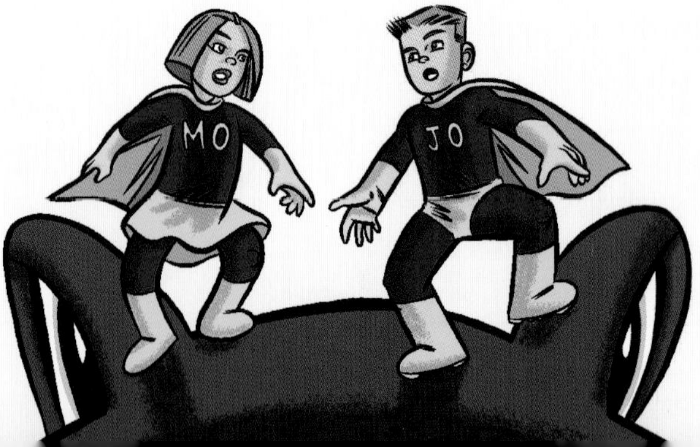
MO
JO